For Keith
S.G.

HAMISH HAMILTON CHILDREN'S BOOKS

Published by the Penguin Group
27 Wrights Lane, London W8 5TZ, England
Viking Penguin Inc., 40 West 23rd Street, New York, New York 10010, U.S.A.
Penguin Books Australia Ltd, Ringwood, Victoria, Australia
Penguin Books Canada Ltd, 2801 John Street, Markham, Ontario, Canada L3R 1B4
Penguin Books (N.Z.) Ltd, 182–190 Wairau Road, Auckland 10, New Zealand

Penguin Books Ltd, Registered Offices: Harmondsworth, Middlesex, England

First published in Great Britain 1985 by
Hamish Hamilton Children's Books

Reprinted 1986, 1987, 1988
Text copyright © 1985 by Sally Grindley
Illustrations copyright © 1985 by Anthony Browne

British Library Cataloguing in Publication Data

Grindley, Sally
Knock Knock! Who's there?
I. Title   II. Browne, Anthony
823'.914[J]   PZ7
ISBN 0-241-11559-0

Printed in Great Britain by
Cambus Litho Ltd, East Kilbride

Knock Knock Who's There?

by Sally Grindley
Illustrated by Anthony Browne

Hamish Hamilton · London

KNOCK KNOCK
Who's there?

I'm a great big GORILLA
with fat furry arms
and huge white teeth.

When you let me in,
I'm going to hug your breath away!

Then I WON'T let you in!

KNOCK KNOCK
Who's there?

I'm a wicked old WITCH
with a long pointed hat
and a wand full of magic.

When you let me in,
I'm going to turn you into a frog!

Then I WON'T let you in!

KNOCK KNOCK
Who's there?

I'm a very creepy GHOST
with a face as white as a sheet
and chains that jangle and clank.

When you let me in,
I'm going to SPOOK you!

Then I WON'T let you in!

KNOCK KNOCK
Who's there?

I'm a fierce scaly DRAGON
with smoke up my nose
and fire in my mouth.

When you let me in,
I'm going to cook you for my tea!

Then I WON'T let you in!

KNOCK KNOCK
Who's there?

I'm the world's tallest GIANT
with eyes like footballs
and feet like a football pitch.

When you let me in,
I'm going to tread on you!

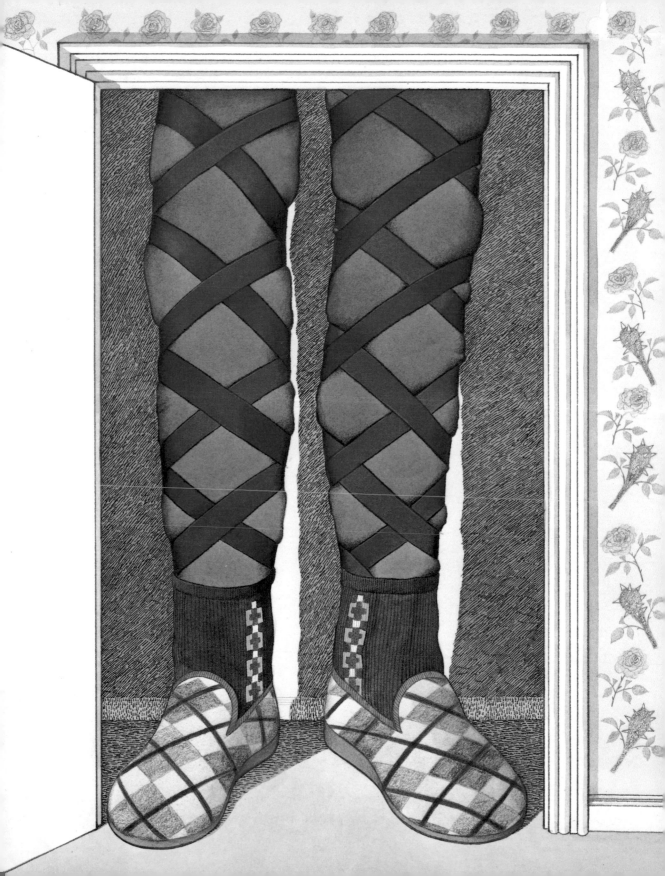

Then I WON'T let you in!

KNOCK KNOCK
Who's there?

I'm your big cuddly daddy
with a mug of hot chocolate
and a story to tell.

PLEASE may I come in?

COME IN, COME IN, COME IN,

There's been a gorilla at the door,
and a witch
and a ghost
and a dragon
and a giant
and . . .

I knew it was you . . . really.